Ladybird Readers

Fairy Friends

Picture words

Rose the fairy

Lily the fairy

mouse

bird

cat

Patch the elf

Lily is a fairy and Rose is a fairy, too.

Lily and Rose like helping their friends.

Lily sees a bird.

"We can help that bird," she says.

Lily and Rose help the bird.

Rose sees a cat.

"We can help that cat," she says.

Lily and Rose help the cat.

Lily sees a mouse.

"We can help that mouse," she says.

It is not a mouse! It is Patch, a bad elf.

Patch likes playing games with people.

15

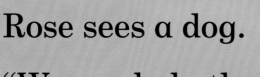

Rose sees a dog.

"We can help that dog," she says.

Lily and Rose help the dog.

16

But it is not a dog. It is Patch the elf again! He is playing a game with Lily and Rose.

"Please go, Patch!" say Lily and Rose. "You are a bad elf!"

Lily sees a fairy.

"We can help that fairy," she says.

"That is not a fairy," says Rose. "That is Patch. Please go, Patch. You are a bad elf!"

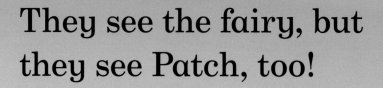

They see the fairy, but they see Patch, too!

"It IS a fairy," says Rose.

"We can help you," says Lily to the fairy.

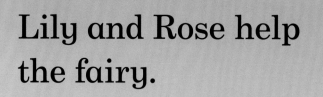

Lily and Rose help
the fairy.

"I can be a bird!"
says Patch. And he
helps the fairy, too.

Lily and Rose are happy.
Now, the fairy is their
new friend.

And Patch is their
friend, too.

Activities

The key below describes the skills practiced in each activity.

🖊 Spelling and writing

📖 Reading

💬 Speaking

❓ Critical thinking

✺ Preparation for the Cambridge Young Learners Exams

1 Look and read. Put a ✓ or a ✗ in the boxes.

1   This is Rose the fairy.   ✓

2   This is Patch the elf.   ☐

3   This is a cat.   ☐

4   This is Lily the fairy.   ☐

5   This is a mouse.   ☐

2 Circle the correct sentences.

1

a Lily is a fairy.
b Lily is an elf.

2

a Patch the elf has got yellow hair.
b Patch the elf has got glasses.

3

a The cat is orange.
b The cat is black.

4

a Lily and Rose help the mouse.
b Lily and Rose help the bird.

3 **Look and read. Write *yes* or *no*.**

Lily sees a bird.

"We can help that bird," she says.

Lily and Rose help the bird.

8

1 Lily and Rose like helping their friends.   yes

2 The bird is Lily and Rose's friend.

3 The mother bird has got four baby birds.

4 Lily and Rose help one of the baby birds.

5 The mother bird is happy.

4 **Look at the letters. Write the words.**

1   r d b i

b i r d

2   y f r a i

....

3   o u m s e

....

4   g d o

....

5   t c a

....

32

5 **Ask and answer the questions with a friend.** 💬 ❓

Lily sees a bird.

"We can help that bird," she says.

Lily and Rose help the bird.

8

1 *How many baby birds are there?*

There are five baby birds.

2 What are Rose and Lily doing?

3 Why are Lily and Rose helping the bird?

4 Would you help the bird? Why / Why not?

6 **Look and read. Choose the correct words, and write them on the lines.**

the cat   orange   Rose   sad

1 Who sees a cat?   Rose

2 Who can they help?   ....

3 Is the cat happy or sad?   ....

4 What color is the cat?   ....

34

7 Find the words.

l c a t i t m o u s e n t h b e n b i r d e r f r t s t r n k d o g e y w y n z b u f f a i r y r a e s

cat

fairy

bird

mouse

dog

35

8 Circle the correct words.

1 (**Who**)/ **What** likes helping their friends?

2 **What** / **Where** do Rose and Lily see in the tree?

3 **Is** / **Are** there five baby birds?

4 **What** / **Where** color is the cat?

5 **What** / **Where** is the white mouse?

9 Who says this?

Patch   Lily   Rose

1 "We can help that bird,"
says ___Lily___.

2 "We can help that cat,"
says _____.

3 "We can help that dog,"
says _____.

4 "Please go, Patch!"
say _____
and _____.

5 "I can be a bird!"
says _____.

10 **Look and read. Choose the correct words and write them on the lines.**

Rose sees a dog.

"We can help that dog," she says.

Lily and Rose help the dog.

dog   birds   glasses   Lily

1 Rose sees a _dog_ .

2 _____ and Rose help the dog.

3 The dog is wearing _____ .

4 There are four _____ .

11 **Order the story. Write 1—5.**

.... Patch plays a game again. He is the dog!

.... Lily and Rose help the cat.

.... Rose, Lily, and Patch help the fairy.

........1........ Lily and Rose help the bird.

.... Patch the elf plays a game. He is the mouse!

12 Match the two parts of the sentences.

1 Lily sees a

2 "That is not a fairy," she

3 "That is

4 Patch is not a fairy. He's

5 Patch likes playing games with

a Patch," says Rose.

b fairy.

c Rose and Lily.

d says.

e an elf.

13 Write *like, likes, does not like,* or *do not like.* 📖 ✏️

1 Rose and Lily ⸺ like ⸺ helping their friends.

2 Rose ⸺⸺⸺ the baby bird.

3 Lily and Rose ⸺⸺⸺ Patch the elf. He is a bad elf.

4 Rose ⸺⸺⸺ Patch's games. "Please go, Patch!" she says.

41

14 **Ask and answer the questions with a friend.** 💬

1 *Which animals are Lily and Rose's friends?*

The bird, the mouse, and the cat are Lily and Rose's friends.

2 What does Patch the elf like doing?

3 Do Lily and Rose like the mouse and the dog?

4 What are the mouse and the dog wearing?

15 Do the crossword.

Down

1 She is a fairy.

2 "We can help that
.........................,"
Rose says.

4 She is a fairy, too.

Across

3 "It is not a
.........................!
It is Patch."

5 "We can help that
.........................,"
Lily says.

16 **Read the questions. Write the answers.**

They see the fairy, but they see Patch, too!

"It IS a fairy," says Rose.

"We can help you," says Lily to the fairy.

1 Is the new fairy wearing glasses?

Yes, she is.

2 Has the new fairy got purple hair?

3 Does Rose say, "It IS a fairy."?

4 Can Rose and Lily see Patch, too?

17 Circle the correct pictures.

1 Who is a fairy?

a

b

2 Who is Lily and Rose's friend?

a

b

3 Who is not Patch?

a

b

4 Who is Patch?

a

b

18 Write *help*, *helps*, or *helping*.

1 Lily and Rose .... help .... the bird.

2 Lily and Rose like .... their friends.

3 "We can .... that cat," says Rose.

4 Lily and Rose .... the fairy.

5 Patch .... the fairy, too.

19 **Write the sentences.** ✏️

(Lily) (Rose) (help) (fairy) (and) (the) (.)

1 Lily and Rose help the fairy.

(can) ("I) (a) (bird,") (be)

2 ....

....

says Patch.

(too) (He) (fairy,) (the) (helps) (.)

3 ....

(are) (Lily) (happy) (Rose) (and) (.)

4 ....

Level 1

Anansi Helps a Friend
978–0–241–25409–7

Cinderella
978–0–241–25407–3

The Enormous Turnip
978–0–241–25408–0

On the Farm
978–0–241–25413–4

Cars
978–0–241–28354–7

Jon's Football Team
978–0–241–25411–0

The Magic Porridge Pot
978–0–241–25406–6

In the Garden
978–0–241–26220–7

Fun with Old Things
978–0–241–26219–1

Fairy Friends
978–0–241–28351–6

Peter Rabbit Goes to the Island
978–0–241–25415–8

Topsy and Tim Go to the Zoo
978–0–241–25414–1

Topsy and Tim Go to the Farm
978–0–241–28355–4

The Fair
978–0–241–28357–8

Daddy Pig's Old Chair
978–0–241–28356–1

Now you're ready for Level 2!